P9-CQE-800

Good Morning, City

STORY BY **Pat Kiernan** · PICTURES BY **Pascal Campion**

FARRAR STRAUS GIROUX · NEW YORK

To Al and Carol, for all the times they read to me. To Dawn, for greeting this book and every project with enthusiasm. To Lucy and Maeve, for always being eager to hear a story. And to New York, for waking up with me.
—P.K.

For Katrina, Lily, Max, and Colin. I love you all.
—P.C.

Farrar Straus Giroux Books for Young Readers
175 Fifth Avenue, New York 10010

Text copyright © 2016 by Patrick J. Kiernan
Pictures copyright © 2016 by Pascal Campion
All rights reserved
Color separations by Embassy Graphics
Printed in China by Toppan Leefung Printing Ltd., Dongguan City, Guangdong Province
First edition, 2016
1 3 5 7 9 10 8 6 4 2

mackids.com

Library of Congress Cataloging-in-Publication Data

Names: Kiernan, Pat, 1968– | Campion, Pascal, illustrator.
Title: Good morning, city / Pat Kiernan ; pictures by Pascal Campion.
Description: First edition. | New York : Farrar Straus Giroux, 2016. | Summary: "A picture book about how the different inhabitants of a city wake up and start their day, from the popular NY1 morning news anchor, Pat Kiernan"—Provided by publisher.
Identifiers: LCCN 2015030874 | ISBN 9780374303464 (hardback)
Subjects: | CYAC: City and town life—New York (State)—New York—Fiction. | Morning—Fiction. | New York (N.Y.)—Fiction. | BISAC: JUVENILE FICTION / Business, Careers, Occupations. | JUVENILE FICTION / Health & Daily Living / Daily Activities. | JUVENILE FICTION / Lifestyles / City & Town Life.
Classification: LCC PZ7.1.K545 Go 2016 | DDC [E]—dc23
LC record available at http://lccn.loc.gov/2015030874

Our books may be purchased in bulk for promotional, educational, or business use.
Please contact your local bookseller or the Macmillan Corporate and Premium Sales Department at
(800) 221-7945 ext. 5442 or by e-mail at MacmillanSpecialMarkets@macmillan.com.

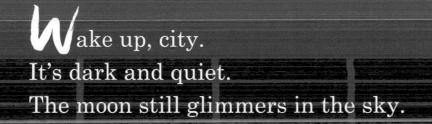

Wake up, city.
It's dark and quiet.
The moon still glimmers in the sky.

It's busy inside the bakery.
Measure. Mix. Knead.
Fresh bread will soon rise like the sun.

A newspaper carrier rushes to her last deliveries.
Whoosh. Thump.
The paper lands on the stoop.

"Drop that rope!" the captain hollers.
Splash. Toot! Toot!
The ferry boat starts its morning rounds.

Wake up, city.
Dogs out walking. Joggers out running.
Dawn's first light peeks through the tree branches.

The delivery truck brings fresh food to the market.
Rumble. Rumble.
The driver greets the grocer with a crate of eggs and milk.

Parked cars become moving cars.
Beep! Beep! Honk!
A police officer keeps traffic flowing.

The waitress welcomes hungry diners.
Clink. Clink. Ring!
Order's up. Breakfast is on the way.

Wake up, city.

Trains screech overhead. People scurry down below.

The sun's long rays break over the tops of tall buildings.

Trash bags are piled up high.
Crash! Smash! Bang!
The garbagemen load the giant truck.

The bus driver sits behind the wheel.
Vroom! Vroom!
Soon it's time for school.

The construction crew is hard at work.
Whack! Bang! Thwack!
They'll build that wall by lunchtime.

Wake up, city.
A child opens her eyes,
as sunlight floods her room.

Across the hall, her baby brother wakes.
"Mama! Dada!"
He's ready to play.

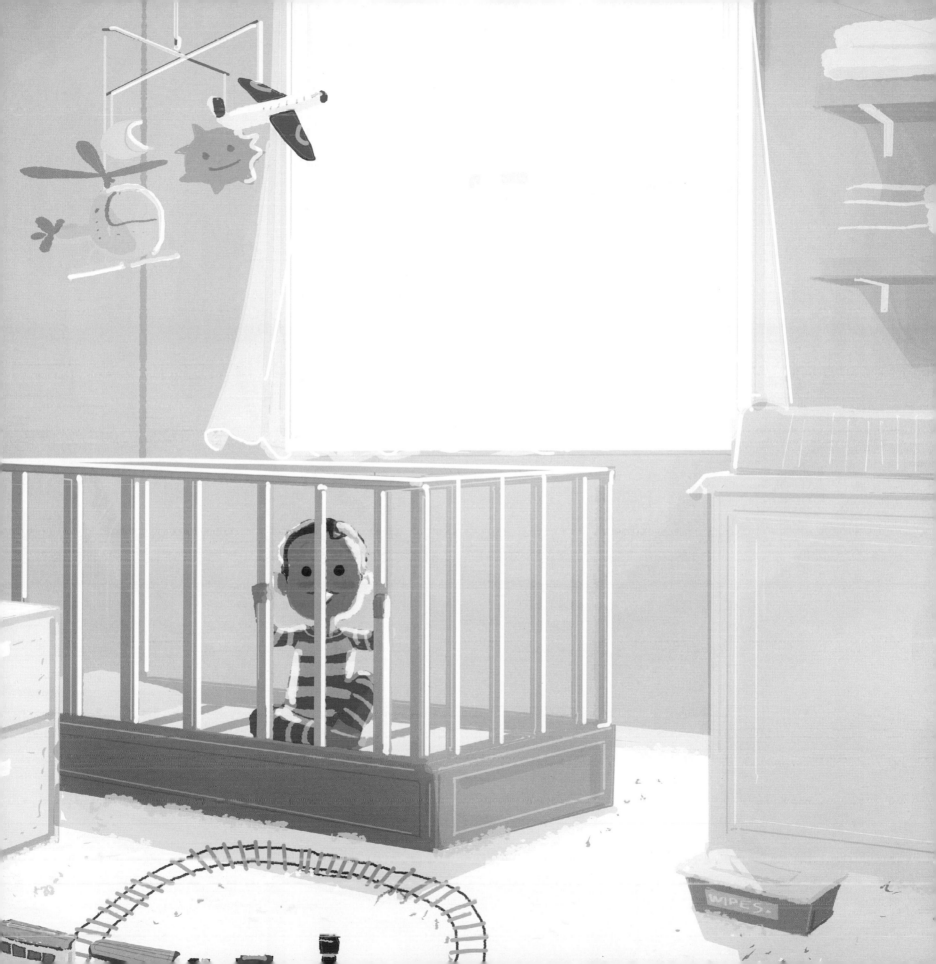

The smell of coffee fills the home.
Drip. Drip. Sizzle.
Pancakes and bacon are hot and ready.

Good morning, city.
The anchorman reads the news.
"It's going to be a beautiful, sunny day."